To my family. Thank you for the writing time. I love you.

And to José Alberto Gutiérrez, for sharing his love of books with the children of La Nueva Gloria.

And to the students of Truman Middle School, for allowing me the same privilege. —A.B.K.

For my love, Alejandro. Thanks for filling our house with books. —P.E.

A portion of the proceeds from this book will go to José Alberto Gutiérrez's foundation, La Fuerza de las Palabras.

Special thanks to Dr. Kristina Lyons of the University of Pennsylvania for her assistance with the project

Text copyright © 2020 by Angela Burke Kunkel
Jacket art and interior illustrations copyright © 2020 by Paola Escobar

All rights reserved. Published in the United States by Schwartz & Wade Books, an imprint of
Random House Children's Books, a division of Penguin Random House LLC, New York.

Schwartz & Wade Books and the colophon are trademarks of Penguin Random House LLC.

Visit us on the Web! rhcbooks.com

Educators and librarians, for a variety of teaching tools, visit us at RHTeachersLibrarians.com

Library of Congress Cataloging-in-Publication Data
Names: Kunkel, Angela Burke, author. | Escobar, Paola, illustrator.
Title: Digging for words: José Alberto Gutiérrez and the library he built / Angela Burke Kunkel; illustrated by Paola Escobar.
Description: First edition. | New York: Schwartz & Wade Books, [2020] | Includes bibliographical references. | Audience: Ages
4–8. | Audience: Grades K–1. | Summary: In Bogotá, Colombia, young José eagerly anticipates Saturday, when he can visit
the library started by José Alberto Gutiérrez, a garbage collector, and take a book home to enjoy all week. Includes note about
Gutiérrez's life and Bogotá. Identifiers: LCCN 2019043235 | ISBN 978-1-9848-9263-8 (hardcover) | ISBN 978-1-9848-
9264-5 (library binding) | ISBN 978-1-9848-9265-2 (ebook) Subjects: LCSH: Gutiérrez, José Alberto—Juvenile fiction. |
CYAC: Gutiérrez, José Alberto—Fiction. | Libraries—Fiction. | Books and reading—Fiction. | Bogotá (Colombia)—Fiction. |
Colombia—Fiction. Classification: LCC PZ7.1.K84637 Dig 2020 | DDC [E]—dc23

The text of this book is set in 16-point Brandon Grotesque.
The illustrations were rendered digitally.

PRINTED IN THE UNITED STATES OF AMERICA
10 9 8 7 6 5 4 3 2
First Edition
Random House Children's Books supports the First Amendment and celebrates the right to read.

"I have always imagined Paradise will be a kind of library."
—Jorge Luis Borges

DIGGING

FOR

Words

José Alberto Gutiérrez and the Library He Built

written by Angela Burke Kunkel

Illustrated by Paola Escobar

schwartz & wade books • new york

In the city of Bogotá, in the barrio of La Nueva Gloria, there live two Josés.

Little José stirs in his bed. The early-morning light wakes him. He was dreaming of Paradise. It is Friday, he realizes with a sigh. *Almost* Saturday.

Until Saturday, he can
ride his bike to school.

He can sit and listen to
Maestra as best he can.

He can play fútbol with his friends.

The day stretches out
before him, like the streets,
like the hills, tomorrow a wish
he knows will come true.

In the same neighborhood, a few streets away, another José understands long days, too. He left school as a boy, his mamá unable to afford it, and went to work as a bricklayer, digging earth with his hands, placing brick after brick until nothing became something. A wall, a building, a home. Still, he read with his mamá, every night. Un cuento at the end of a long day felt like Paradise.

Now, in the early-evening light, as the first José
rides his bicycle home, his mamá calling him for dinner,

the second José gets ready for work. He prepares his garbage
truck for its route through the wealthier neighborhoods of Bogotá.

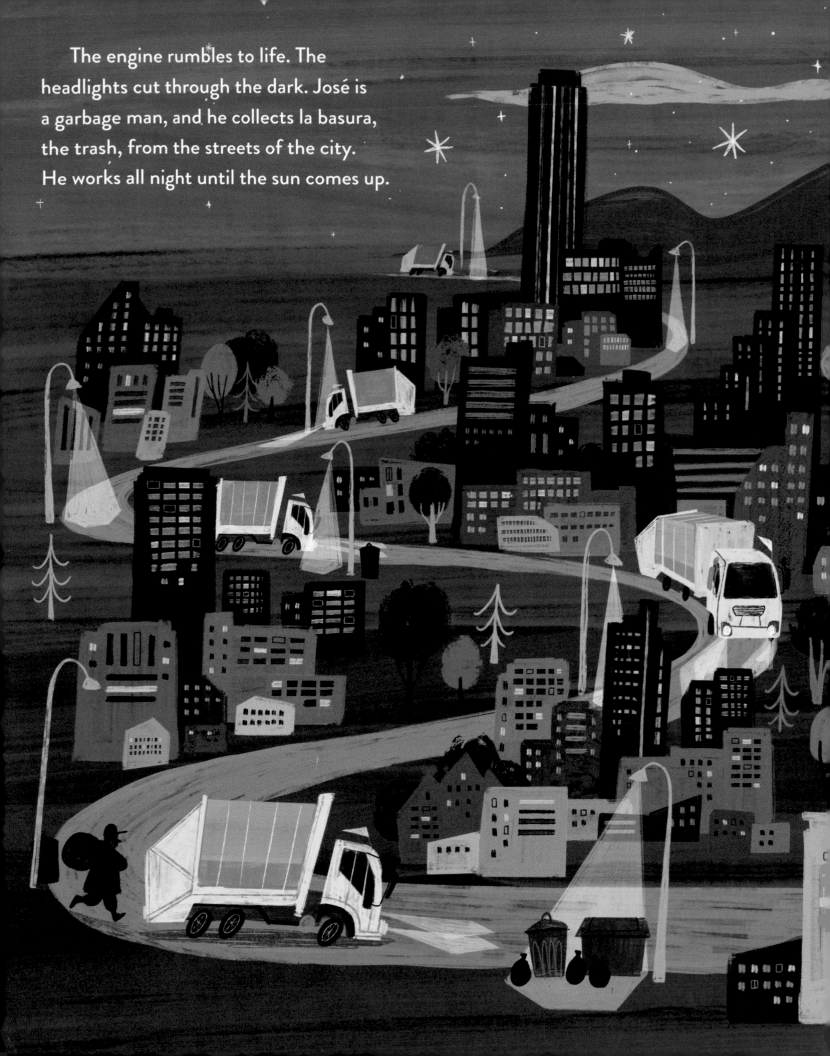

The engine rumbles to life. The
headlights cut through the dark. José is
a garbage man, and he collects la basura,
the trash, from the streets of the city.
He works all night until the sun comes up.

José scans the sidewalks as he drives, squinting in the dim light. He searches the household trash for hidden treasure . . . books! Some are stacked in neat piles, as if waiting for José. Others take a bit more digging. José doesn't mind.

He digs now because of el primer libro, that first book, found long ago. When José first began work as a garbage collector, he spotted a thick novel in the trash—*Anna Karenina* by Leo Tolstoy. He dug it out and read it again and again, always opening to a faraway time and place full of steam trains, ballrooms lit by candlelight, sleighs gliding through snow. He found other books and read those, too. Each was different, each its own world to discover.

Finally, Señor José is finished with his route. The garbage truck winds its way through the wide streets, back to the more crowded part of the city, back to the garage. In the cab, next to him because it is precious cargo, rides a stack of almost fifty books—thin, thick, worn, almost new. It is a stack making a journey to join other stacks. An encyclopedia of animals A to Z, a book of fairy tales, a long novel, well-loved. They all ride home next to José, their pages vibrating along with the rumble of the engine.

José walks home from the garage. He pauses on the step to
unlock the door, balancing books in the crook of his arm.

A few pages to read, a few hours to dream, and then it is a new day. Tonight, he revisits Macondo, a magical village deep in the jungles of Colombia, and he is lost in a place where time moves by its own rules.

At last, it is Saturday, Saturday, Saturday!
Little José's legs carry him as fast as they can.
As he runs through the neighborhood, other children
join him. It's like a race, but they all will win.

His feet touch the step of Paradise at last.
Señor is waiting to greet them, smiling, as
he does every Saturday.

José enters Paradise to find stacks and stacks of books, stacked like the homes of their neighborhood. Libros rescued by Señor José. Everywhere, every corner, is stuffed with them. Picture books for niños. Classic stories, thick, with elegant covers. Big textbooks, heavy with their complicated subjects.

José stays a long time, traveling among the high stacks, afraid to disturb them, hesitant to dig. Señor comes to find him. He holds up a book and smiles.

Señor sits. José sits. The barrio quiets. The book opens.

It opens to a place beyond the barrio, a place José cannot ride his bicicleta to. With each turn of the page, both Josés see something new—something different from the same streets and the same hills.

Digging leads to more digging.

At last, little José makes his own selección with a nod and a shy smile and a "Gracias" to Señor, and he's off, his feet flying back home, his hands flying through chores, through dinner, through washing his face and behind his ears so he can climb into bed and inspect his new libro and devour the cuento inside, even warmer and more satisfying than his dinner.

In the early-morning light, little José stirs in his bed. The book is tucked under his pillow. He devoured it again in his sueños, dreaming of a lonely planet, a flower, a boy, a fox, the journeys they make.

It is Sunday, he realizes with a sigh. He has to wait again, a whole week.
Waiting in bed for the sun to rise. Waiting for his friends to come and play.
Waiting once again for Saturday. Waiting for Señor to open his doors,
where the libros sit, waiting on their shelves. Waiting for José to find them.

AUTHOR'S NOTE

Over ten million people live in the city of Bogotá, Colombia. There are only nineteen libraries. There was no library in La Nueva Gloria barrio until 2000, when José Alberto Gutiérrez took matters into his own hands.

A lifelong Bogotá resident, Gutiérrez is a former garbage collector who is known as the Lord of the Books. Early in his career, Gutiérrez found a discarded copy of *Anna Karenina* on his route. He describes that discovery as the "little book [that] set the flame and this snowball that never stopped rolling." Today, in addition to running his library, Gutiérrez directs the foundation he established, La Fuerza de las Palabras (The Strength of Words), which provides reading material to schools, organizations, and libraries across Colombia. His efforts have earned worldwide recognition, including features in the Colombian newspaper *El Tiempo* and *U.S. News and World Report*, on BBC News, and more. Gutiérrez has also addressed global audiences—twice at the Guadalajara International Book Fair, and at the Austrian Literacy Association's annual conference.

Gutiérrez himself went back to school in his fifties. It took him three years to earn his high school diploma, but in building his library, he empowered himself as well as others. "Lots of people mocked me," he says. "They would laugh when they found out about my project. But now, twenty years later, they are amazed. My dream is to exchange my garbage truck for a truck full of books and travel the country. I am sure I will pull it off."

José on his nighttime route

Children browse the library in José's home

AP Images / Fernando Vergara

AP Images / Fernando Vergara

FEATURED BOOKS

While researching this story, I came across several references to books that have been especially meaningful to Señor Gutiérrez. The following are showcased in the illustrations:

• The first book Gutiérrez discovered on his garbage route was **Anna Karenina** by Leo Tolstoy, a novel about an upper-class woman who feels trapped by her everyday life. The book is set in nineteenth-century Russia, a time and place quite different from modern Colombia.

• **One Hundred Years of Solitude,** by Nobel Prize–winning Colombian author Gabriel García Márquez, is the multigenerational story of the Buendía family and their lives in the isolated village of Macondo. It is an example of magical realism, in which events mirror everyday life, with the exception of some fantastical (and often unexplained) elements.

• The book young José reads at the end is Antoine de Saint-Exupéry's novella **The Little Prince.** First published in 1943, it is considered a children's classic, featuring a young explorer who visits Earth after living alone on a tiny planet no bigger than a house. Also a complex allegory, the story mirrors the author's experiences leading up to World War II and explores larger questions about love and the meaning of life.

SELECTED ONLINE SOURCES

La Fuerza de las Palabras: lafuerzadelaspalabras.org/site/

"Bogota's Bibliophile Trash Collector Who Rescues Books": aljazeera.com/indepth/features/2017/05 /bogota-bibliophile-trash-collector-rescues-books-170522084707682.html

"Colombia's 'Lord of the Books' Saves Tomes from the Trash": csmonitor.com/World/Americas/2018/0625 /Colombia-s-lord-of-the-books-saves-tomes-from-the-trash

"From Garbage to the Bookshelf": facebook.com/watch/?v=910112349130273

"'Trashy' Books: Garbage Collector Rescues Reading Material for Colombian Children": usnews.com/news /world/articles/2015/08/26/colombian-garbage-collector-rescues-books-for-children